My Father Always Embarrasses Me

Written by Meir Shalev

Illustrated by Yossi Abolafia

WELLINGTON PUBLISHING
Chicago

My Father Always Embarrasses Me

From the Hebrew original Aba 'ośeh bushot
translated by Dagmar Herrmann

Copyright © 1988 by Keter Publishing House, Jerusalem, Ltd.
English translation copyright © 1990 by Dagmar Herrmann

Published in the United States of America in 1990

Wellington Publishing, Inc.
P.O. Box 14877
Chicago, Illinois 60614

Library of Congress Cataloging-in-Publication Data

Shalev, Meir
[Aba 'ośeh bushot, English]
My father always embarrasses me / written by Meir Shalev;
illustrated by Yossi Abolafia;
[translated by Dagmar Herrmann]. 32 pp.
Translation of: Aba 'ośeh bushot.
Summary: Mortimer finds that everything his father does
embarrasses him until the day he enters a baking contest in
Mortimer's class.
[1. Fathers and sons — Fiction.] I. Abolafia, Yossi, ill.
II. Title
P27.S52813My 1990
[E] — dc20   89-27709

ISBN 0-922984-02-6

Typeset in Sabon by Presentation Management Inc., Chicago
Printed and bound in Italy

Down the street lives Mortimer Dunne.
His mother is a television reporter.
Mortimer thinks the world of her.
His father is a writer.
He does nothing —
only hammers away at the typewriter
and embarrasses his son.

At the pool, Mortimer's dad
never dives into the deep end.
He crawls around on all fours,
wearing his wide-brimmed hat.

Mr. Dunne loves to play football,
but he always runs the wrong way
and helps the other team score.
At PTA meetings he snores
in front of all the other moms and dads.
In restaurants, he walks straight to the kitchen
to peek into pots and pans.

At the wedding of Aunt Lenore
he wore his favorite shorts.
Worst of all,
he gave his son that awful name,
Mortimer.

Mortimer's mother always gets up early,
grabs her coffee, skims the paper,
and says, "Honey, go wake up Dad.
He'll take you to school.
It's getting late."
With a quick kiss, "bye,"
and a toss of her hair,
she is gone for the day.

Mortimer's father likes to sleep at least until eight.
Mortimer knows he'll be late for school again.
Already he hears himself reciting the old line:
"Sorry, I'm late. My father did not wake up on time."

Finally at eight fifteen,
with a squint and a yawn,
Mortimer's father starts
looking for his clothes,
mumbling,
"I'm sure I left everything right here...
Or perhaps over there!"
That's slightly more than Mortimer can bear.
"I've told you a thousand times," he groans,
"lay out your clothes before you go to bed!"

Every day Mr. Dunne takes Mortimer to school.
On the way he tells him stories
he wrote the night before.
Suddenly on Main Street he starts
singing at the top of his lungs.
Mortimer is so embarrassed,
he doesn't know what to do.
"Can't you sing softly?" he asks.
Father ignores his plea and sings full blast.
Passersby stare.
Mortimer begs, "Stop singing, please! Let me go!
Just drop me off right here!"
But his father takes him all the way to the door.

"Now how about a kiss?" says Mr. Dunne, bending down.
Mortimer is upset.
"I'm late! I can't!" he says, "Not now!"
Alas, it's no use, for his father persists
(and all the children hear):
"If you won't give me a kiss,
I'll just find another kid who will!"

"You won't believe how Dad behaves!"
complains Mortimer to his mom.
"In front of all the children at school
he embarrasses me! It's not fair!"
With a smile, Mother says,
"Well, what can we do, honey,
your father loves kissing a lot, and besides,
you have to learn to live with what you've got!"

The other day,
Mr. Dunne took Mortimer to the movies
and let him invite two friends.
When the movie got really scary,
he covered his eyes,
ducked his head, and whispered,
"I can't watch them when they shoot each other!
Tell me when it's over, please!"
(Would you believe that's what he said?)

It was awful.
Mortimer didn't know what to do.
"Don't even ask what Dad did to me today,"
he said to his mom, in tears.
"Now everyone will say
that my dad is a scaredy-cat!"

Every night, before he falls asleep,
Mortimer lies in bed listening
to the music from the radio
and the clicking of his mother's heels
on the glistening bare floor.
From out in the street he hears a honking car.
A cat squeals in the neighbor's yard.
In the kitchen, the freezer hums.
There is another sound that keeps Mortimer awake:
the pounding of the typewriter,
as his father types stories
deep into the night.

Yesterday, Mortimer's teacher suggested
that they have a party and invite the parents.
The mothers could enter a baking contest,
and the one who baked the loveliest cake
would win a prize.
At home, Mortimer's mother said at once,
"I'm too busy, honey. Here, take some money, go
buy a cake, or, better yet, talk it over with Dad."

Mortimer's eyes filled with tears.
His father winked. "Cheer up!" he said merrily.
"Everything will be all right!
I'll go without typing tonight and whip up a cake
that will win us first prize!"
All night long Mr. Dunne baked.
He woke Mortimer at seven, to show him the cake.

Mortimer felt sick.
He rolled his eyes and thought to himself,
"Why does my father always embarrass me?"
In his hands his dad held something
that was the size and color of an automobile tire.
On his head was perched a chef's white hat.
He glanced into the mirror, smiled,
and briskly said to Mortimer, "Up and at 'em!
Let's go for it!"

On the table, the cakes were out of their boxes.
All the fathers were sitting in the back, except for
Mr. Dunne who was up front with all the mothers
and the wheel of a cake that looked quite obnoxious.

Jane's mom had baked an apple strudel.

Moody's mom had made cupcakes with pink frosting.

The flaky puffs that Pete's mom had brought were still hot from the oven.

Mrs. Stroll had made a delicious chocolate roll.

A frosted gingerbread tower
stood proudly before Mrs. Mabel.

But all eyes were on Mortimer's father
in his chef's white hat
and his wheel of a cake that took up half the table.

The teacher started sampling the goodies.
You could hear her "oooh" and "aaah"
as she kept smacking her lips.
At last she came to Mr. Dunne's cake,
stopped in her tracks and stared at the wheel.
(Mortimer was mortified.
What an awful mess! Oh dear!)

"Allow me to cut you a slice, ma'am,"
Mortimer's father said politely, with a little bow.

He barely touched the cake, in a secret spot,
and suddenly it was frosted with chocolate!
Out of the middle popped twenty red strawberries!
As he gently tapped the sides,
a gush of velvety filling spread throughout.
He then flicked his finger at the top,
and a sugar rose burst open
on a dollop of caramel cream.
"Wow!" the kids cried.
The parents were knocked flat.
And the teacher asked Mortimer's father:
"Where did you learn to do that?"

He answered: "From my father.
He was the very best baker in our town.
All day long he did nothing but bake
sweet rolls and bread, and especially cakes.
He never did anything else.
Except, well... he always embarrassed me.
You see, Brad's father was an officer.
He wore a fancy uniform.
Susie's father was the manager
of a large hardware store.
Tom's father was a carpenter,
but my father was just a baker.
I was so ashamed of his tall white hat
that I used to hide it.
My father understood, and didn't mind it at all."

Mortimer felt happy,
but also a little ashamed of himself.
"Come on, my son," his father said,
"let's go now, but please hold my hand,
for I'm afraid to walk home alone."
The teacher smiled, the children cheered,
and so did all the moms and dads.

And Mortimer?
He stood on his tiptoes,
hugged his father, and gave him a kiss.

He wasn't embarrassed at all.